How's Harry?

**If you enjoy reading this
<u>MAMMOTH READ</u> try:**

Ghost Blades Anthony Masters
Delilah Alone Jenny Nimmo
Charlie's Champion Chase Hazel Townson

How's Harry?

Steve May

Illustrated by Philip Hopman

Mammoth

For H, a gentle soul

First published in Great Britain 1996
by Methuen Children's Books Ltd
Published 1997 by Mammoth
an imprint of Reed International Books Ltd
Michelin House, 81 Fulham Road, London SW3 6RB
and Auckland, Melbourne, Singapore and Toronto

Reprinted 1997 (twice)

Text copyright © 1996 Steve May
Illustrations copyright © 1996 Philip Hopman

The rights of Steve May and Philip Hopman to be identified as
author and illustrator of this work has been asserted by them in
accordance with the Copyright, Designs and Patents Act 1988

ISBN 0 7497 2830 2

J6
MAY

A CIP catalogue record for this title
is available from the British Library

Printed and bound in Great Britain
by Cox & Wyman Ltd, Reading, Berkshire

Contents

1. No !

Mr Robbins said no. 'And when I say no, I mean no.'

Kate said, 'Oh, but, Dad — '

'Don't "oh, but, Dad" me,' replied Mr Robbins, 'I'm dadamant.'

Kate turned to her mother.

'Don't look at me,' said Mrs Robbins. 'I hate rats.'

'I don't want a rat, I want a hamster. Plea-ease! I'd look after it and everything!'

'Hamsters and rats are all rodents,' said Mr Robbins, 'and we're not having none of them.'

'He's a pig, your dad,' said Anne.

Kate nodded glumly, watching the hamster run up and over her friend's hands.

'Can I have a go?'

'It isn't a go!' said Anne. 'Harry's an animal, not a toy.'

Anne had two hamsters: Harry, who was running over her hands now, and Harriet, who was a bit fat and lazy and nibbled your fingers if you stroked her.

'I'm going to let them mate,' said Anne. 'Then I can sell the babies. The pet shop pays a pound each — '

'I want one!' moaned Kate.

'You're welcome to have one,' replied Anne, 'and as you're a friend, I'll only charge you fifty pence.'

That evening, after washing up, and doing her homework, and running an errand to the shops, and making a cup of tea for her mum, Kate told her dad about Harriet and Harry and Anne's plans for mating them.

'Fascinating,' he said, with a yawn. 'What's all that to me?'

Kate took a deep breath. 'Can I please have one of the babies?'

'They're called cubs,' said Mr Robbins.

'Can I have one of the cubs, then? They're only fifty pence.'

Mr Robbins sighed, and laid aside his newspaper, and stretched his legs, and wiggled his toes in his sheepskin slippers.

'We've been all through this before, and money is not the thing,' he said. 'Looking after an animal is a great responsibility. It's like having a child. And, as with parenting, there are times when you're dad-tired, and you don't want to be bothered. And it is at those times, that a sense of duty, not love, is what drives you on.'

'Is that a yes or a no?' Kate asked, impatiently.

Mr Robbins frowned, and thought for a moment. Then smiled. 'My dear, I'm afraid it's a dadfinite no.'

'I'm not giving up,' Kate told Anne.

Anne said, 'Pass the sawdust.'

Kate did as she was told. Harriet, bigger than ever, waddled over Kate's foot and away under the bed.

'I'm going to have one of Harriet's babies,' Kate said.

'I don't know,' said Anne, 'It depends how many there are.'

'But you promised!'

'Yes, but Mandy's having one, and Naomi, and Jo, and then if there's any with special colours I'm going to keep them for breeding, 'cos if they're special colours like smoked pearl you can get pounds and pounds.'

Kate's heart bulged with envy, and desire. 'OK, but if there's more than three, and he's not a special colour?'

'We'll see.'

'I really don't mind if it's not very pretty-looking, or if it's lame or something.'

'All right, don't keep going on! If there's more than three, you can have one. Bedding.'

Kate passed the shredded paper. It felt hard and uncomfortable. Her hamster would have soft furry bedding, like cotton wool.

'What about your dad, though?' Anne asked. 'How are you going to persuade him?'

'Just leave that to me.'

'Pretty impressive, pretty impressive indeed,' said Mr Robbins, laying aside the folder. The folder was labelled: *Outline for My Hamster*, and on the front was a drawing of a hamster, traced from a book. Inside, there were four sheets titled *Cost*, *Care*, *Characteristics*, and *Benefits*.

'Well?' demanded Kate.

'You've certainly done your homework.'

'And a very nice little picture,' added Mrs Robbins.

10

'But — '

'But what?'

'But no. And before you run screaming from the room — '

Kate stopped in the doorway, eyes wet, throat tight. Her dad was smiling, nodding like a puppet.

'Katie, my dear, if you put a stop to all this rodent nonsense, I'll make you a dolly house. I can't say fairer than that, can I?'

Mr Robbins smiled. Kate did not. She had stopped playing with her dolls some time ago.

Mr Robbins was busy explaining how dolls are much better than hamsters. 'They don't bite and they don't smell, and you can still practise being grown up, looking after them.'

Kate strode from the room, slamming the door. Her father called after her. 'Very grown up, I must say. Very grown up indeed. If that's the way you treat doors, Lord knows what you'll do to a small furry animal.'

Mrs Robbins said to her husband, 'It is very natural for a child to want a small pet to look after. It's part of growing up.'

'I'm not stopping her *wanting* one,' replied Mr Robbins, 'I'm just stopping her *having* one.'

While Mr Robbins worked on the dolly house, Kate saved her pocket money. She bought secret supplies of sawdust, soft bedding, and hamster food.

'If he won't *let* me, he can't *stop* me,' she

told Anne.

She even found a cage. It was in the cupboard in Miss Simmons' room at school, and Miss Simmons said Kate could have it, because she was never again going to bother with classroom pets.

'They're more trouble than they're worth, especially in the holidays.'

The cage was blue metal, and a bit rusty in the corners, but it had a wheel and a food tray that slotted in the side. Kate smuggled it into the house and hid it on top of her wardrobe behind the spare pillows. Then, she waited.

2. Harry

Kate missed the birth. Anne didn't tell her till the next day, at school.

'Are the cubs all right?'

'Fine, fine,' said Anne, checking her lip-gloss.

'And Harriet?'

'A bit grumpy.'

'And how many are there?'

'Three.'

That evening, Kate went to see them. The baby hamsters were tiny, strange, and not very cute. Pink, hairless, with red bits. Eyes gummed shut. Kate counted them carefully, several times, in case Anne had made a mistake, and missed one.

Three in all.

'What are their names?'

Anne thought. 'Harvey, Henry and Harold, I suppose,' she said.

Harriet fussed around, grumpily letting the cubs suckle.

'Don't touch them or she'll eat them,' Anne warned.

Kate tried to smile. 'Does Jo still want one?'

'Yes, Jo still wants one.'

'And Naomi?'

'Yes.'

'And Mandy?

'And Mandy. They've all paid, in advance.'

'Have they been round yet, to see them?'

'Not yet. Best to keep them away till the babies've got their fur. Otherwise, some people get put off.'

Not me, thought Kate.

Jo chose Harvey, and renamed him Harold, but before he got used to his new name, she dropped him on the kitchen floor. He survived the fall, but not the cat. The cat ended up with a scratched nose, but Harvey ended up inside the cat. Jo asked Anne for her money back, but Anne refused.

14

'He wasn't guaranteed against getting eaten,' she said.

Naomi chose Harold, and renamed him Henry, but left the top of his cage open, and by morning Henry had gone.

'Mum thought she could hear him scratching under the floorboards, but Dad says that's a proper rat.'

Mandy chose Henry, and renamed him Harvey. Mandy's brother Colin (six) thought Harvey was great. For a treat, he launched him in a model aeroplane from his bedroom window. The plane crash-landed in a neighbour's flower-bed, and Harvey was never seen again.

'Well,' said Kate, 'when I get my hamster, he certainly won't be flying in any aeroplanes.'

'I don't know,' said Anne. 'I expect Henry enjoyed it at the time. And they deserve every bit of excitement they can get. They have such short little lives.'

'How short?' Kate asked.

Anne flipped a page in her magazine. 'Well, as a rule, two years, but Harriet only lasted one.'

'What? Harriet – she's dead?'

Anne nodded, not taking her eyes off the magazine. Kate couldn't believe her ears.

'What did she die of?'

'I'm not sure.' Anne licked her fingers, turned another page. 'The other day I looked into her cage, and when I prodded her, she didn't move.

15

Her body was all cold and stiff in a bendy sort of way.'

'What did you do with her?'

'I put her in a plastic bag and popped it down the waste-disposal chute.'

Kate choked back her anger and tears. 'How about Harry?'

'Oh, he's fine. I'm hoping to sell him as soon as possible. Trouble is, he's got this yucky skin disease at the moment, and that puts people off.'

'Let me see him!' Kate demanded.

Anne groaned. 'OK, after *Neighbours*.'

'Forget *Neighbours*. Let's go *now*.'

Harry wasn't visible, but his nest shuddered and twitched every now and then. Anne, wearing rubber gloves, plucked the hamster out of his nest. He didn't open his eyes. His fur was wet-looking, plastered down flat, and under it the skin was blotchy. Anne made a face, and plopped Harry down in the middle of her desktop. He did not move, but sat there, breathing in little gasps, his flanks shivering.

Kate leaned her face close to him. 'What's actually wrong with him?'

Anne shrugged. 'Search me. I just hope it isn't catching.'

'Have you taken him to the vet?'

'Not yet.'

'Why not?'

'Well, I keep meaning to.' Anne made a face.

16

'Thing is, you need a little box to put them in, don't you? And we haven't got a little box, and every time we *do* get a little box, it gets thrown away before I remember what I wanted it for.'

'I thought you loved hamsters.'

'I did. I used to. But I think I've grown out of them, now.'

Kate bit back angry words, and offered to take Harry to the vet herself, this minute.

'Sure,' said Anne, peeling off the gloves, and offering them to Kate, 'but if it's more than one fifty, forget it.'

'You stinge!'

'Come on. Even in perfect condition, I'm not

going to get more than two quid for him.'

When the vet saw Harry, she whistled softly to herself. 'My, my, you do look poorly.'

Kate shifted awkwardly. In the waiting-room she had read the *Schedule of Fees* over and over again. Cheapest seemed to be 'euthanasia without consultation . . . £5.50'.

'I'm afraid,' she stammered, 'I'm afraid cost could be a problem.'

'Don't you worry about that,' said Miss Kopinsky, busily probing at the animal's fur and skin with her pale fingers. 'Let's put this one down to medical science, shall we? I've never seen a hamster in this condition before, so it'll all be new and trail-blazing.'

She chose a white powder, which she dissolved in water, then sucked up in a dropper. She showed Kate how to hold Harry by the fold of skin at the back of his neck, and force the dropper into his mouth. He did look cute! His head all scrunched, eyes tight shut, his little paws grasping at thin air, and his teeth fighting the dropper, until finally, unable to resist, he gulped down the medicine.

'Do you think you can do that?' asked Miss Kopinsky.

'I reckon so,' replied Kate. 'How often?'

'Twice a day for four days. Then bring him back. And don't hesitate to come in sooner if he gets any worse.'

Kate kept up the treatment faithfully, which wasn't easy, especially on school days. It meant she had to keep calling at Anne's house, not to see Anne, but to see her pet.

'Honoured, I'm sure,' Anne said. 'Do you want me to leave the room, so you can be alone with him?'

It was touch and go, but after two more visits to Miss Kopinsky, and vitamins, Harry made a full recovery.

'Totally cured,' Kate announced proudly to Anne, lifting a sleek, wide-awake Harry out of the shoebox by his armpits.

'Great,' replied Anne. 'Now all I've got to do is find a buyer.'

Kate watched the small animal sniffing and twitching on her palm.

'How much do you want?' she asked.

3. Yes!

'So, he's second-hand *as well*,' said Mr Robbins, peering into the cage.

'Yes, but he *was* cheap,' Kate lied. In fact Anne, once she realised how eager Kate was to buy Harry, had raised the price to £3. Kate paid up.

'What's more,' continued Mr Robbins, 'you've gone over my head and behind my back. If I was a proper father, and good to my word, I'd give this little fellow his marching orders pretty sharp quick.'

Kate swallowed at the lump in her throat. Harry, asleep, snuffled in his new fur-style bedding.

'However,' Mr Robbins went on, 'the fault is yours, not his. The sins of the owners should not be taken out on the pets.'

'So I can keep him?'

Mr Robbins wrinkled his nose.

'What a dreadful old cage,' he said. 'All small and rusty. I tell you what.' And he went out on his bike, and came back an hour later with a new cage, made of tough plastic, with metal bars, and an exercise wheel.

'Do you like your new cage?' he cooed to Harry.

'It's not a cage,' Kate said, 'it's a house.'

'Soppy old so-and-so!' Anne said. 'I thought he was supposed to be all foot-down and heavily against.'

'Yes,' replied Kate, 'so did I.'

Every day after school, Kate woke Harry up, and got him out, and let him run round the living-room floor. Mrs Robbins was not best pleased.

'Where is he now?' she'd ask.

'He's got to have some exercise,' Kate argued.

'That's right,' agreed her father. 'Even in prison they get an hour's exercise in the yard.'

'He's not in prison, he's a pet,' Kate complained.

'I don't care what he is,' said her mother, 'I don't like him scuttling over my foot. I can't concentrate on the telly.'

'He won't hurt you,' her husband assured her. 'He's a very gentle little chap.'

'And,' Kate added, 'he's got perfect markings, a rounded face, and straight whiskers.'

'And huge teeth!' cried Mrs Robbins. 'Get him away from there!'

Harry, head upside-down, jaw stretched wide, was chewing at the under-edge of the door.

'Don't you worry,' her husband assured her.

'Once he's finished, I'll go over the teeth marks with my felt-tip pen.'

When Kate had taken Harry back upstairs, Mrs Robbins said, 'That girl, she takes better care of that animal than she does of herself.'

Her husband nodded, and sniffed. 'So it should be. And I intend to make daddle sure she continues so to do.'

'He's watching us all the time,' Kate told Harry. Harry didn't seem to be listening. He was busy sliding ever so gradually down the side of the bed, clinging by his rear toenails.

'Silly!' Kate said, catching him just in time.

'That's a big drop and a hard floor.'

But when she put him back on the bed, Harry went back to exactly the same spot on the duvet, and did exactly the same thing. Rescuing him again, she held him so near her face she could feel his whiskers on her nose.

'Won't you ever learn? You'll hurt yourself sliding into the unknown like that. What if it was a big valley? You'd fall miles.'

'It's because they don't have valleys in Syria, where he comes from,' explained Mr Robbins' head, which had appeared round the door.

'Can't you read?' asked Kate, pushing Harry back into his house. She'd stuck a large notice on her bedroom door: 'VERY PRIVATE. KNOCK AND WAIT.'

'How's Harry, then?' Mr Robbins asked.

'Fine,' Kate replied. 'About the same as he was five minutes ago, the last time you asked.'

'Good, good, good,' said Mr Robbins, strolling to the side of the cage, into which he peered.

'Warm enough, old chap?' he asked, raising his voice.

Harry, busy with his bedding, teasing and tearing it, did not reply.

'Looking after you all right, is she?' Mr Robbins went on.

'No!' exclaimed Kate. 'I'm poisoning him and torturing him!'

'. . . seventeen, eighteen, nineteen.'

23

Mr Robbins took the pencil from behind his ear, and noted the number in his notebook.

'Nineteen what?' Kate asked.

'Droppings,' sniffed her father. 'There were only thirteen last time I looked. And the sawdust in the toilet area's on the wet side of damp, I'd say.'

'And that is the end of the news,' said Kate, trying not to scream.

'Because,' Mr Robbins explained, bobbing his head from side to side, 'hamsters are very clean little creatures, and they only smell if their owners neglect them. See you soon.'

The door clicked shut behind him.

'Pig!' shouted Kate.

'But the novelty does soon wear off,' Anne said, next time she came round.

Kate said, 'Maybe, but Harry's like an old friend, now. He's part of the room. It wouldn't be the same without him.'

'It certainly wouldn't,' Anne agreed, wrinkling her nose, and sniffing.

4. Smells

Mrs Robbins noticed the sour smell when she went into Kate's room to hoover.

'It might just be these old socks stuffed down the side of the bed,' she told her husband.

'No!' crowed Mr Robbins, sniffing triumphantly. 'The smell undoubtedly arises from the rodent's housing conditions. You see – thirty-seven droppings! The novelty's worn off, and she's started to neglect her pet.'

'There's no need to sound so pleased about it, Derek.'

'I'm not pleased, I'm shattered,' gloated Mr Robbins, circling the cage, hands clasped behind his back.

When Kate got back from Anne's house, Mr Robbins asked, 'How's Harry?' ten times in seven minutes. The first nine times, Kate answered, 'Fine', or 'Absolutely fine.' The tenth time, she exploded.

'It's none of your business, Harry's my pet. I take good care of him, and if you don't think so, you can have him, make him your pet, so you can look after him.'

'It may come to that,' Mr Robbins replied, 'but the question *now* is: when did you last clean him out?'

'Yesterday! I do it every day!'

And Kate ran to her bedroom, and threw herself on to the bed, and cried. Then she stopped crying and sniffed.

No doubt about it.

There *was* a smell.

She began to think back. It *seemed* like yesterday she'd last cleared Harry's cage of wet sawdust and droppings. But it wasn't yesterday. Yesterday she'd gone round to Jess's, and the night before she'd had gym club, and the night before that was always good on telly, and the night before that she'd come in very tired after hockey, and the night before that and the night before that she couldn't remember, but if you worked it out on a calendar, it was two weeks at least since she'd changed any of the sawdust.

Come to think of it, she couldn't remember the last time she'd *fed* him!

She took the lid off the cage, and poked at the nest. The nest gave a little start.

'So you're alive, then,' she said.

Eyes closed, ears flat, Harry pushed his head out of the bedding. Kate picked him up, and fondled him, and wet him with her kisses and

tears, till he looked a bit like he used to when he was ill.

'I didn't mean to neglect you,' she said. He didn't seem to blame her. He was too busy trying to find a way off her jumper, down her jeans, and on to the floor. Every time he got past her knees, she scooped him up, and put him back on her jumper again.

'I'm going to clean you out properly tomorrow,' she told him.

For now, she scooped up the dampest corner of sawdust, and covered the patch with fresh sawdust, and spooned out as many droppings as she could into a plastic bag. Then she sprayed the room with her mum's perfume.

Then she put Harry back in his house, and went and watched *Top of the Pops*.

'How's Harry?' asked Mr Robbins, out of the corner of his mouth.

'Fine,' replied Kate.

'It still stinks in here,' Anne said, when she called round next day.

'Don't you start,' moaned Kate, spraying more perfume into the air. 'I'm going to clean it out properly tomorrow.'

Anne shook her head, and took a couple of skipping steps across the room.

'I'm so glad I got rid of my hamsters. It's great, not having to worry about feeding and cleaning and everything. And it's so peaceful at night – no gnawing and clanking. I'm never going to have children.'

'Come off it,' said Kate. 'Children are a bit different.'

'No,' said Anne, 'they're the same as pets but worse, 'cos if you drop them near a cat they don't get eaten. They're useless, they really are, and if you say anything to them they cry.'

Anne's mum had just had another baby.

'Harry doesn't cry,' Kate said, getting a word in at last.

Anne, peering into his cage again, said, 'He doesn't do much at all, does he?'

'He does, in his own way.'

'Like what?'

Kate shrugged and tutted. 'That's just the way they are, hamsters. You can't expect him to sing and dance, can you?'

Anne sniffed again. 'He certainly hums. Why don't you sell him?'

'No way!'

'Mandy's desperate for another one. You could screw her for at least a couple of quid.'

'No!'

'And the medical-research station at Long Compton, they pay even better. Mind you, they only buy by the dozen. Trevor Brain, he breeds mice specially. Have you seen his new mountain bike? That was paid for entirely out of vivisected rodents.'

Harry's nest quivered.

'Don't say things like that!' Kate said. 'He'll hear you.'

'Don't be silly,' said Anne. 'Hamsters don't understand English. That's why they're such dumb pets. They never even know you're there. They can't love you. They don't appreciate what you do for them. Just like babies.'

'Oh, come on,' Kate said. 'Let's forget hamsters and babies and watch the film.'

But Mr Robbins was in the front room, and he wouldn't let them watch the film. He insisted on watching a programme about zoos instead.

'Da-ad,' Kate complained, 'we don't want to watch this.'

'I don't suppose the animals want to be in the zoo, either,' he replied.

Ann tugged Kate's sleeve, but Kate couldn't tear herself away. The pictures were horrible, but she couldn't stop looking. There were mangy lions and paranoid polar bears and glowering gorillas. The worst bit was a chimp who kept hissing and throwing himself at the glass of his cage. A woman kept saying; 'Is it right to keep these wild animals in captivity?'

5. Dreams

That night Kate had a dream. In the dream, she'd forgotten to do something. Trouble was, she couldn't remember what. Then a demon dressed up as a zoo-keeper told her, 'It's Harry. You haven't fed him for seven years.'

'Where is he?' asked Kate, in the dream.

'In a locked room at the end of a long dark corridor.'

The zoo-keeper sounded just like her dad.

Dreading what she'd find, Kate crawled to the locked door, and opened it.

At first, she didn't recognise Harry, because he'd grown so big. He was over two metres tall. Being well-mannered, he had tried to stay in his cage, which he wore squeezed on to the top of his head like a hat. Also, he'd learned how to talk.

'Because you forgot to turn the telly off, and I've picked it up from that.'

Kate woke, in a panic. She ran to Harry's cage, and reached into his nest, and pulled him out. He was normal size. Feebly, his legs cycled. His eyes stayed shut. His body was hot and soggy. She cradled him on her palm, covering him with her other hand. He settled at once, curled up, fast asleep. He had not woken.

Maybe that was good. It would be easier to talk.

'What are we going to do?' she whispered. 'All this time, I've pretended you live in a house, and we're friends, but the plain fact is, it's a cage, and you're a prisoner. I don't want to keep you in captivity. But if I let you go, you won't have a chance, because of the climate, and because you're so tame and trusting you'll just get eaten.'

Harry shuddered in her hands, and lifted his head, and sniffed. His eyes were still shut.

'What I'm saying is, I don't want to carry on like

we have been, I want to make things better for you.'

Her father's head appeared round the door. 'For a start you could give him a proper clean-out.'

Kate snarled and flung a shoe.

The head withdrew.

The worst thing was, her dad was right.

She put Harry carefully into the dolly house. Then she spread newspaper on the floor, emptied all the damp sawdust on to it, and all the droppings; washed the cage with steaming hot soapy water (even the awkward corner bits) and mopped it dry with an Irish-linen tea towel ('It was all I could find,' she told her mum); then she

sprinkled new sawdust in, and filled the food bowl to overflowing with fresh vegetables and her mum's peanuts.

'Well done,' said Mr Robbins, peeping in round the door, without knocking. 'That's much better.'

'Go away,' said Kate.

She lifted Harry out of the dolly house, put him on her palm. Although his ears were still flat, and his eyes were still shut, he sat up on his back legs, and began to wash his face, running his paws up and over behind his ears.

'Oh, you are sweet,' she cried, kissing his flat ears.

'I may look sweet to you,' he replied, 'but all I'm doing is what comes naturally. This is my normal in-the-wild behaviour. The fact that you find it sweet is really neither here nor there.'

He had stopped cleaning himself, and was now waddling round her hand, looking for a way off. Ungrateful little ratbag! She put him down on the carpet. After a motionless moment, he scurried away under her bedside table. Kate crouched down beside the table.

'I don't suppose you actually know what I am, do you?' she asked.

Harry had to admit that he wasn't sure.

'Are you a pair of pink fur-less animals with five legs, and a thick long tail?'

'You need your eyes tested.'

'Not really,' Harry protested. 'I've got excellent

eyesight, for a hamster. But it's really designed for night-work – owls and shadows, and hawks crossing the moon; in daylight I can't tell a bat from a belfry at more than a centimetre.'

Kate held her hand out, close to his nose.

'This isn't a fur-less animal,' she explained. 'This is my hand, like your paw. Understand?'

Harry sniffed the hand, then peered vaguely up at Kate. 'And the tail?'

'That's my arm – and this is my sleeve, my clothes.'

'And the universe is mainly made of clothes?'

'Not really. What makes you think that?'

'Because once I get on to the clothes part, it seems to last forever – it doesn't matter how far or how fast I run, I never reach anywhere else.'

'That's because I keep picking you up and putting you back where you started from.'

'Why do you do that?'

'To stop you escaping.'

'Oh.' Harry thought for a bit. 'What about the rest of you?'

Kate put her hand flat on the floor next to Harry.

'Climb aboard,' she said.

Harry sniffed the hand, warily.

'Come on, get a move on!'

'I'm sorry, but I always have to sniff things first.'

And he sniffed her hand again, before cautiously waddling on to it.

35

She lifted him up so he was on a level with her eyes.

'This is my face,' she told him. She breathed out gently through her mouth. He blinked, drew his head into his shoulders.

'That was my breath,' she explained.

'Does it always smell like that?' he asked.

She thought. 'Not always. I had a garlic-bread pizza for tea last night.'

Harry nodded, sadly. 'I've always wondered what pizzas were like, but I'll never know.'

'Why not?'

'Because hamsters hate pizzas.'

'How do you know?'

'It says so in all the books.'

'It used to say in books the world was flat.'

'Isn't it?'

Kate ran to the kitchen. She got a tissue, and picked the last thick crust bit of pizza out of the bin.

'What are you doing?' asked her mother.

'It's for Harry.'

'Hamsters don't eat pizza.'

'They do in some countries. I saw it on *Blue Peter*.'

Which convinced Mrs Robbins.

Harry was less easy to please.

'So this is pizza?' he said, sniffing the crust warily.

'Well, yes, part of it.'

36

'It smells of tea bags.'

'Ah, well, that's because it's been in the rubbish bin.'

She brushed a couple of tea leaves off the piece of pizza. Harry rested one of his paws on the crust.

'What's worrying you?' Kate asked.

'You said, it's been in the bin.'

'So?'

'Wouldn't that worry you?'

'Yes, but I'm a human being, and you're a rodent, and rodents, they're used to eating muck out of rubbish tips, aren't they?'

'You're thinking of rats and mice. I'm a golden hamster, and I come from Syria where there are no rubbish tips, but the wide and beautiful desert.'

Kate interrupted him. 'But, Harry, just about all the food you've ever eaten is reject stuff – unfit for human consumption: lettuce with the sell-by up, best-before carrots, and as for the nuts and seeds and things —'

'Nice to know you care,' said Harry.

'I mean, it's good,' Kate hurried on, 'being able to eat anything. I wish I could!'

'What's stopping you? You can help yourself to the red dog-biscuit bits in my bowl any time you like.'

Kate dropped the pizza in her waste bin, and changed the subject. 'There's something else I wanted to talk to you about: housing. I mean, is your house big enough?'

'A cage is a cage however big it is.'

'I'm sure if you saw a bigger house – like the one Mandy bought for Henry. It's like a palace, with playrooms and passageways and goodness knows what else.'

Harry tutted. 'Why should a big house make me happier?'

'Because you'd have much more room, to run about.'

'Happiness comes from inside. If you aren't happy with yourself, where you live won't make any difference.'

'But it can help, can't it?'

'Well,' said Harry kindly, 'if it makes *you* feel better, go ahead and buy me a mansion.'

Kate stifled a howl. 'It isn't what *I* want, it's what *you* want.'

Harry drew back his head, then twitched his nose. 'No one ever asks hamsters what they want.'

'There's always a first time. I'm asking, what do you want, to improve your quality of life?'

'How about less red dog-biscuit in my feed?'

'Yes,' snarled Kate, 'I've already made a note of that, but I'm talking about what you really really want in your heart of hearts to do with your life.'

Harry sat very still on her palm. 'It's not the kind of thing I've ever thought about. All I'm used to doing is eating and sleeping and going to the toilet.'

'If you could just give me some idea, then I could help you achieve your aims.'

'OK.' Harry cleared his throat. 'I hear there's a place called the Long Compton Research Station, where rodents take part in experiments at the cutting edge of science. Maybe I could go there, and play some humble role in the progress of learning?'

Kate shook her head. 'Not a good idea.'

'I know I'm not brilliant brain-wise, but I wouldn't expect to be a boffin, not straight away. I'd be quite happy making the tea, or anything really, so long as I was part of the effort.'

Kate tried to think of a gentle way of explaining. 'At Long Compton, you wouldn't be part of the effort, you'd be the effort itself.'

'How do you mean?'

'They cut you up.'

Harry's shoulders twitched. 'Why?'

'To see how you react.'

'I can tell you that now. I wouldn't care for it one little bit.'

Kate hurried on. 'Not that I want to dictate your life to you. If you really want to go to Long Compton, I'll see if I can arrange it. Thing is, they only take rodents in dozens, so I'd have to try and organise a party —'

'Don't trouble yourself,' interrupted Harry.

'You know, I'd always assumed that science was meant to be good for everyone.'

'It is, in the long run,' Kate replied. 'When they cut you up, they don't mean it personally.'

'Oh,' said Harry, 'that's all right, then.'

'Any other ideas?' ventured Kate, trying to sound bright.

'Any chance of me cutting up a few scientists?'

'I'm afraid not. For a start, you haven't got big enough hands. And if you *could* learn to hold a knife, it'd take for ever, a little hamster like you chopping up a fat old scientist – even if we could get him to lie down in the first place.'

Kate looked at her watch. *The Brunch Bunch* was on in three minutes.

'Tell you what,' Kate said. 'I'll come back later on after you've had a chance to think.'

And she scooped Harry up and plopped him into the freshly cleaned house.

He went frantic.

He sniffed, he scratched, he scurried.

'What on earth's the matter now?' Kate demanded.

Harry glanced up. 'It's all different. All my smells have gone.'

'Good job too.'

'And my droppings and all my store of nuts and slimy lettuce.'

'I've cleaned it out for you, so it's all nice and fresh.'

Harry lumbered up his ladder. 'And what about my bed?'

He burrowed his nose into the fresh bedding. 'It's all clean and horrible.'

'Hang on, then,' tutted Kate irritably, and ran to the bin, and found some scraps of old bedding, and pushed them in through the bars.

Harry stuffed the material into his pouches, and scuttled back to his bedroom, and started to weave the old bits among the new.

'All right now?' Kate asked.

Harry was too busy weaving and trimming to answer.

So Kate clicked the latch shut on the cage, and left him to it.

But she couldn't concentrate on the TV. All she could think about was Harry, and the things he'd said, and one thing in particular stuck in her mind: 'I come from Syria, where there are no rubbish tips but the wide and beautiful desert.' It was that that gave her the idea. She was so excited she had to rush straight back up to her bedroom and wake Harry up.

'What is it this time?' he asked, poking his nose out of his new bedding.

'I've got a great idea for your future. The perfect answer.'

'It isn't anything to do with medical research, is it?'

'No. It's Syria. Where your great-great-great-great-grandmother came from in nineteen thirty. I'm going to take you back to where your roots are.'

Harry yawned. 'But not today, I hope?'

'No. Of course not today. It takes planning.'

'Good,' said Harry. And curled up again and went back to sleep.

6. Plans

Kate made very careful plans. She'd start off wearing her warmest, oldest clothes for the journey across England and western Europe, but once it started getting hotter, she'd throw these clothes away, or give them to poor people, so she didn't have to be bothered with carrying them.

They could sleep in youth hostels, or bed and breakfasts, or even barns, like they do in books, if it was warm enough, and there weren't any dogs.

'What a dad-um stupid idea,' sneered Mr Robbins, arms crossed, leaning in the doorway, watching her pack.

'Well, we might not bother with the barns,' Kate said, folding her swimsuit.

'Haw, haw, haw, haw, haw,' sniggered her father, shaking his head. 'I bet you anything you like, you won't get further than Vince's Happy Shopper.'

'We'll see about *that*,' spat Kate, spinning round, glaring. But her father had gone, chuckling down the stairs.

The bedding stirred again in the hamster's cage, and Harry's head emerged.

'Do you think he might have a point?' he asked.

'Oh, do shut up,' Kate hissed.

'What's so special about Syria?' Anne asked, when she called round the next day.

Kate, while she prepared her equipment, explained. 'It says in my book that every single golden hamster in this country today is descended from a single litter of twelve cubs found in a burrow in Syria in nineteen thirty.'

Anne wasn't impressed. 'It seems a long way to go to see a burrow.'

'That's not the point,' said Kate. 'The point is, Harry's got his heart set on it.'

'No, I haven't!' Harry shouted.

Anne jumped. 'He never shouted when I had him.'

'Maybe you didn't listen.'

'I'm really not that fussed,' Harry protested, standing up with his nose squeezed through the bars of the cage. 'I'd just as soon stay here.'

'No you wouldn't,' Kate told him.

Harry appealed to Anne. 'Just because her father says it's stupid, she's got to show him he's wrong.'

'It's nothing to do with my dad,' Kate insisted. 'I'm doing it for Harry, and it's my duty to respect

his wishes as much as my own, because we're both animals.'

'Even if he's off his trolley?'

'It's not me who's bonkers!' Harry complained.

Kate ignored him. 'In hamster terms, going to Syria's a very natural ambition.'

'How are you going to get there?' Anne asked.

'On foot.'

'And ratbag?'

'In my pocket. Till we get to the desert. Then he can scuttle.'

'You must be mad,' Anne told her, shaking her head.

When Anne had gone, Harry said, 'Maybe she's got a point.'

'Don't start that again. It's like pizza: you won't know if you like it unless you try it.'

Harry, thinking of medical research, said, 'There's some things I'd rather not try, thanks.'

But Kate didn't listen. She'd had another idea. A way to show Anne, and her father, that she meant business. She reached into the cake, and lifted Harry out. His back legs flurried.

'We're not going right this minute, are we?' he asked. 'Because I've got lots of little things I need to do first.'

'No. We're going to have a practice run. To see how you cope with travelling.'

'Where are we going? Paris?'

'No. The park.'

7. Out...

Kate carried Harry loose in her donkey-jacket pocket.

'OK?' she asked.

'Fine,' replied Harry. He couldn't see anything, but he could hear and smell a lot.

'Is that a tiger?' he asked, as they passed Mrs Grime's cat on the wall of number twelve. The cat sniffed and stared.

Then they turned on to the main road. It was the rush hour. Cars zoomed, a bus rumbled past. Heels clattered, people jostled. Everywhere was the smell of haste, of urgency.

Kate put her hand into her pocket. Harry was shivering.

'OK?' she asked.

A fat motorbike belched alongside.

'What sort of animal is that?'

Before Kate could reply, a siren erupted suddenly out of nowhere, loud-er, LOUD-ER, *LOUD—*

Too much for Harry. He was wriggling and

struggling against the thick wool prison, trying to escape.

Kate backed into the doorway of Vince's Happy Shopper, and opened the top of the pocket. As the light hit him, Harry froze. Kate put him on her palm, level with her face, and asked him what the matter was.

He sat there, motionless apart from the quivering of his flanks, and the occasional start as his heart beat unexpectedly.

Stroking his back, Kate tried to soothe him. 'Cars are what people use to go to work, or in fact, to go anywhere. Like your wheel – I know you don't use it, but if you did, it would be very similar to a car, in the sense that when you run in it, you think you're getting somewhere. The only difference is, in a car, you actually do get somewhere. Unless the traffic's very bad. OK now?'

'How much farther is it to the park?'

'That's it over there.'

Harry squinted. 'And how much farther is Syria?'

'We've walked about half of one mile. Syria is another two thousand.'

'What's a thousand?'

Kate had to think. 'A thousand is – there's a thousand ones in a thousand.'

'So it's a lot?'

'Think droppings when I haven't cleaned your cage – house out for a month.'

Harry whistled through his teeth. 'That is plenty!'

They turned into the park. Children were playing on the swings. Harry sniffed.

'Nice,' he said. 'But I can't wait to get home. I'm going to chew my bars and move my bed.'

A raindrop caught him on the flank, and he started. 'Can we go now, please?'

Kate said, 'Harry, there's something I haven't told you. We're not going home tonight. We're going to practise sleeping rough.'

Harry gulped. 'Is that strictly necessary?'

'It's like training. If we can do it one night, we can do it as often as it takes to get to Syria. It'll make people take us seriously.'

'Where's my nest?'

'In your cage, at home. I'm not carrying *that* around in my pocket.'

In the distance there was the sound of a breaking bottle. A dog barked. The light was fading. Trees loomed and leaves swished in the wind. Harry cleared his throat. 'I think I'd prefer to go home.'

Kate snorted. 'Just as I thought. You're not a golden hamster, you're yellow.'

'Don't talk dog-biscuit,' he replied. 'If I had a cage and a bed I'd be happy to sleep anywhere.'

'That's the whole point,' snapped Kate. 'For you *not* to have a cage.'

And she pushed Harry down into her pocket, and set off along a path.

'Where are we going now?' Harry asked.

Kate was about to say, 'Back home!'

But it was too late. Her path was blocked.

8. ...and Back

'Hello, darling.' The boy peered into Kate's face. 'You're a bit young to be out on your own, aren't you?'

He took a hissing drag on the stub of his fag, and blew the smoke at her.

'She's not on her own.'

'Who said that?'

'Rodge, it come from down below,' called a girl sitting on a nearby bench. The crowd with her all squealed with laughter.

'It was me,' said Harry, poking his head out of Kate's pocket.

'Who?' asked Rodge.

'In her pocket,' shouted the girl.

'It's a ruddy rat,' laughed someone else.

'A hamster, actually,' said Harry, blinking.

'A talking rat!'

'We'll soon see about that.'

The gang gaggled from the bench, and surrounded Kate. She swallowed hard, and pushed Harry down into her pocket.

'Come on, let's have a look,' said Rodge.
'Where's he gone?'

'I'll find him,' said a blonde girl, with spotty
cheeks. And she tried to force her hand into Kate's
pocket.

'Get off!' shouted Kate, and pulled away. The
others laughed.

'Come on,' said the blonde girl, in a wheedling
voice, 'we only want to have a look.'

'Yeah,' said someone else, 'we ain't never seen a
talking rat before.'

'That's right,' added Rodge, remembering to
elbow himself back to the front. ' 'Cos there's no
such thing.'

Kate was thinking fast. 'Well, if there's no such thing, then there's nothing to see, is there?' and she turned to walk away.

Rodge grabbed her arm. 'If there's nothing to see, show it us.'

'Leave her alone,' said a third girl, pushing through from the back. 'She's only young. Big fat slob like you. Let go of her.' And she brushed Rodge's hand from Kate's shoulder.

'You show him, Sal,' someone said.

'Don't mind Roger,' Sal said to Kate. 'He doesn't really mean it. He's just a pig. But,' she went on, 'you have got a rodent in your pocket, haven't you?'

Kate thought a moment, then nodded.

'I told you so!' squealed the blonde girl.

'Shut up, Debs,' Sal snapped. And then, softly, to Kate, 'Can I see him, please?'

Kate reached slowly into her pocket, and drew Harry out, bundled in her fingers.

'Aaah,' said the girls, in chorus.

'Isn't he sweet!'

'What's his name?'

'Harry.'

Harry had flattened himself on Kate's palm like a sheepskin rug. His nose was on full alert, tense, quivering.

'How many do you need to make a fur coat?' sniggered Roger, but no one laughed.

'We used to have gerbils,' said another boy.

53

'Yeah, but they've got tails,' said someone else. 'We had them at school.'

And they all started talking about their old pets.

'Can I hold him?' asked Sal, gently.

Kate held out her hand. Harry stiffened, flattened himself even flatter. When Sal picked him up his legs circled like four propellers. His white belly was bright in the gloomy air.

Sal lifted him so his face was close to hers, and whispered, 'And do you talk, my furry little friend?'

Harry didn't reply.

Instead, he bit her. On the nose.

Sal screamed, and dropped him, and shouted something. This time, she did not call him her furry little friend.

Roger was hooting with laughter.

'Ninja rodent!' howled someone else.

'If I get my hands on him!' threatened Sal.

But she couldn't get her hands on him, because Harry was nowhere to be seen.

'Well, for goodness sake, look for him!' demanded Kate.

The gang did what they were told. Someone thought Harry had scuttled under a bush, but when they got down on all fours and peered, they couldn't see him.

'It's like looking for sick in a stir-fry,' complained Roger.

Sal crawled round with peanuts in her hand, tweeting with her lips: still no Harry.

Kate decided all these people must be scaring him. 'So please, if you wouldn't mind, go away, just for now?' The gang moaned a bit, but trailed off, leaving Kate alone.

High above, the lamp popped and flickered.

It was dark.

It was cold.

It was late.

Her throat went tight with fear. She wanted to run, run home, back into the warm, safe. See her mum. And dad. Forget Harry. Tell her dad he'd escaped from his cage. The park gates were only fifty metres away. She took two quick strides, then stopped herself. Even though her stomach was churning with panic, she couldn't desert him.

Mustn't.

'He was trying to stick up for you,' she told herself.

She frowned. Where was he? Stupid ratbag.

'Harry, Harry?' she cooed, not very loud, because it sounded thick, and she didn't want to attract any more attention. 'Where are you, ratbag?'

Then she listened.

It was very quiet in the park.

An owl hooted.

In the distance, a bottle smashed.

From the direction of a rubbish bin, came a tiny crack-crack-crack sound. Kate crept to the bin, and bent over. In the gloom, under the bin, she could just make out whiskers, and then beady eyes, and two little paws. The paws held an old potato crisp, which Harry was nibbling, noisily.

When Kate got home, her mum told her off, while hugging her, and asking where she'd been, and making macaroni cheese, and ringing the airport, where Mr Robbins had gone to book a flight to Syria.

'He thought you were serious,' Mrs Robbins tutted, hugging Kate again.

'I was,' mumbled Kate, and pulled herself away, and ran upstairs.

'Are you OK?' Kate asked, after she'd put Harry back into his cage. He did not reply.

He burrowed into his nest, and curled up. Kate waited, and waited. Some time later she heard the crack, crack, crack, as he bit into a peanut.

'Come on,' said her mum, 'come down and have something to eat.'

'I've got to make sure Harry's all right.'

'I'm sure he'll be fine,' said Mr Robbins, who had just arrived back from the airport. 'You take very good care of him.'

'Do I?'

'Yes. And you can't be on duty twenty-four hours a day. If you're overprotective, it'll make his life a misery.'

So Kate went down into the warm kitchen, and had some macaroni cheese, and they all watched telly, and Mr Robbins did not ask, 'How's Harry?'

Not once.

Next day, Anne called round. 'How's things on the

57

Syria front?'

Kate blushed. 'We've had a change of plan.'

'Very sensible.'

'Harry says he's happier staying here.'

In Harry's house, the bedding quivered. Anne leaned over the cage, peering in.

'Happy here, are you?' she asked.

Harry didn't reply.

Anne turned to Kate. 'Not very chatty today, is he?'

'No,' replied Kate, thoughtfully. 'No, he isn't.'

Steve May

CLOSER, CLOSER

Bobby always has her hand up in class. She always gets her own way. Basically, Bobby's good at most things, and what she's not good at she fakes. I'm good at some things, but even the things I'm good at, Bobby's better.

Bobby and Sarah are twins but their relationship is fraught – Sarah constantly feels that she is in Bobby's shadow. But then Sarah meets Jess, and Jess's friends, all people who Sarah's mother would not approve of.

Through Jess, Sarah enters a new world, a world where she no longer feels in Bobby's shadow. But fitting in with her new friends isn't so easy either, and when Sarah goes to the Ashdown festival with them, events take a dramatic turn . . .

By the author of *The Fish Fly Low*, described in the *Guardian* as being written with 'real understanding.'

W. J. Corbett

LITTLE ELEPHANT

Tumf (Short for Tumffington) is the luckiest little elephant in Africa until the terrible day when the ivory poachers make him an orphan.

Tumf sets out on a nightmarish journey but finds friends along the way, including a veagle (a vulture posing as an eagle?), a tortoise and a cheeky little monkey.

Across Africa, through desert and swamp, water and land, happy and sad, Tumf plods on in his quest for happiness.

A funny and touching story by the author of *The Song of Pentecost*, winner of the Whitbread Award.

'The author has a great capacity for endowing his creations with the fancies and foibles we humans recognise as our own. His animals seem to behave just that bit more responsibly . . .'
The Junior Bookshelf

Anne Fine

THE CHICKEN GAVE IT TO ME

Andrew laid it on Gemma's desk. A cloud of farmyard dust puffed up in her face.
  'Where did you get that?'
  'The chicken gave it to me.'
  'What chicken? How could a chicken give it to you? It's a book.'

The book is a chicken's extraordinary tale – *The True Story of Harrowing Farm*. Its scratchy little pages unfold a story that changes lives, the story of a chicken who flies frillions of miles to try and save us humans . . .

A new comic masterpiece from Anne Fine, winner of the Carnegie Medal and the Smarties Award.

'Not since *Animal Farm* have I come across so clever and biting a social fable as this . . . it is difficult to convey the wit and brilliance that sparkle on every page . . . It's topical in its greenness and its theme is presented with a lightness of touch which makes its message palatable to readers of all ages.'
  The Junior Bookshelf

'a terrific little book . . .'
  Joanna Lumley

Andrew Matthews

LOADS OF TROUBLE

'Well, m'lady, the village has got a problem with your . . . er . . .' Councillor Earwacker cast about for words like a man trying to find his slippers in a dark bedroom. At last, inspiration struck him and made his eyes go glittery. 'The village has got a problem with your elephant unmentionables, m'lady!' he announced.

Lady Feeblerick is outraged when her elephants are accused of causing an unsavoury pollution problem. And she is even more outraged when she thinks the elephants will have to go. Will their keeper Toby Hoken and his mysterious assistant Bat be able to save them from certain trouble . . . ?

An hilarious tale of adventure from the author of *Wickedoz, Wolf Pie, Mistress Moonwater* and *Dr Monsoon Taggert's Amazing Finishing Academy* which was shortlisted for the 1989 Smarties Prize.

A Selected List of Fiction from Mammoth

While every effort is made to keep prices low, it is sometimes necessary to increase prices at short notice . Mandarin Paperbacks reserves the right to show new retail prices on covers which may differ from those previously advertised in the text or elsewhere.

The prices shown below were correct at the time of going to press.

☐	7497 1421 2	**Betsey Bigalow is Here!**	Malorie Blackman	£2.99
☐	7497 0366 0	**Dilly The Dinosaur**	Tony Bradman	£3.50
☐	7497 0137 4	**Flat Stanley**	Jeff Brown	£3.50
☐	7497 2200 2	**Crazy Shoe Shuffle**	Gillian Cross	£3.99
☐	7497 0592 2	**The Peacock Garden**	Anita Desai	£3.50
☐	7497 1822 6	**Tilly Mint Tales**	Berlie Doherty	£3.50
☐	7497 0054 8	**My Naughty Little Sister**	Dorothy Edwards	£3.50
☐	7497 0723 2	**The Little Prince (colour ed.)**	A. Saint-Exupery	£4.50
☐	7497 0305 9	**Bill's New Frock**	Anne Fine	£3.50
☐	7497 1718 1	**My Grandmother's Stories**	Adèle Geras	£3.50
☐	7497 2611 3	**A Horse for Mary Beth**	Alison Hart	£3.50
☐	7497 1930 3	**The Jessame Stories**	Julia Jarman	£3.50
☐	7497 0420 9	**I Don't Want To**	Bel Mooney	£3.50
☐	7497 0048 3	**Friends and Brothers**	Dick King Smith	£3.50
☐	7497 2596 6	**Billy Rubbish**	Alexander McCall Smith	£3.50
☐	7497 0795 X	**Owl Who Was Afraid of the Dark**	Jill Tomlinson	£3.50

All these books are available at your bookshop or newsagent, or can be ordered direct from the address below. Just tick the titles you want and fill in the form below.

Cash Sales Department, PO Box 5, Rushden, Northants NN10 6YX.
Fax: 01933 414047 : Phone: 01933 414000.

Please send cheque, payable to 'Reed Book Services Ltd.', or postal order for purchase price quoted and allow the following for postage and packing:

£1.00 for the first book, 50p for the second; **FREE POSTAGE AND PACKING FOR THREE BOOKS OR MORE PER ORDER.**

NAME (Block letters) ....

ADDRESS..

....

☐ I enclose my remittance for...........................

☐ I wish to pay by Access/Visa Card Number

Expiry Date

Signature . . . .

Please quote our reference: MAND